STOP THAT NOISE!

PAUL GERAGHTY

CROWN PUBLISHERS, INC. • *New York*

High up in the great green forest,
the sun began to rise.

Way down in the deep, dark shadows,
a tree mouse was curling up to sleep.

Creech! Creech! Woop! Woop!
chirped the frogs.

The sounds were screechy, the
sounds were sharp: *Woopoo!*
Woopoo! Creech! Creech!

"Stop that noise!" yelled the tree
mouse. "I'm trying to sleep!"

But all she heard was the *Zee-zee-zee-zee!* of a cicada somewhere outside. *Zee-zee-zee-zee!* Then the *Hmmm* of a humming bird— *Hmmm* over here and *Hmmm* over there.

"Stop that noise!" yelled the tree
mouse. "I'm trying to sleep!"

Then *Keeoo…kedik-kedik-kedik!* came
the calls from the forest crown.

Toucans pierced the curtain of green
with a *Keeoo...kedik-kedik-kedik!*

"Stop that noise!" yelled the tree mouse. "I'm trying to sleep!" But the forest was alive with songs and sounds.

Yaag! Screecha-screecha-screecha! squawked a macaw. *Yaag! SCRAAA! SCRAAA!* squawked another.

"Stop that noise!" yelled the tree mouse. "I'm trying to sleep!"

But her voice was drowned out by the monkeys that bickered in the branches. *Duwoop! Ooo-ooo-ooo-ooo!* whooped one. *Yeek! Yeek!* screamed the others.

"Stop that noise!" yelled the tree mouse. "I'm trying to sleep!"

And suddenly the forest fell silent. All she heard was the echo of her own voice.

The animals clung
in silence, not
daring to move or
make a sound.

Even the cats that ruled the forest now cowered in the quiet. That's better! thought the tree mouse.

But it wasn't. She couldn't sleep. The silence grew worse than any noise, until finally she cried out, "Please make some noise! I'm trying to sleep!"

She waited. And then there was a noise. She heard a distant *Brrrm, brrrm*...and then a *C-r-r-r-r-r-r-RACKA-DACKA-RACKA* **SHOONG!** that shook her to the ground.

A tree had fallen. And a gaping
hole was left in the crown of the
great green forest.

C-r-r-r-r-r-RACKA-DACKA-
RACKA **SHOONG!**
Another tree came down!

Brrrm, BRRRM...the ugly sound made the ground shudder. And the tree mouse knew her tree would be next.

She looked up at her home. Then she turned to the terrible sound. And at the top of her voice, she yelled, "STOP THAT NOISE!"

But that noise didn't stop.

Brrrm, it drew closer, *BRRRM*, till the earth thundered; *BRRRM!* it grew louder, **BRRRM!** till the earth shook. But the tree mouse stood firm.

And something made the driver stop. And
when he stopped, he felt the silence. He saw
the broken trees. He saw the fallen nests.

And he sensed angry eyes watching him.

So he sat and he thought. He stayed there
and thought till the sun went down. And
when it was dark, he went away.

And he never came back.

Now way up in the great green forest, the trees are growing again.

And deep down in the dark shadows,
a tree mouse curls up and closes her
eyes. She listens to the songs and
sounds of the forest, which tell her
that, for now, she can sleep in peace.

For Extremely Tiny Most Miniature
and extremely tiny people everywhere

Library of Congress Cataloging-in-Publication Data
Geraghty, Paul.
Stop that noise! / by Paul Geraghty.
p.   cm.
Summary: A tree mouse comes to appreciate the noises of the other
forest animals after hearing the noise of a machine destroying the
forest.
[1. Forest animals—Fiction. 2. Conservation of natural
resources—Fiction.] I. Title.
PZ7.G29347St 1993
[E]—dc20   92-6608
ISBN 0-517-59158-8 (trade)
0-517-59159-6 (lib. bdg.)

10 9 8 7 6 5 4 3 2 1   First American Edition